The
CHRISTMAS
TREE SHIP

A Ship of Joy!
Carol Crane

CAROL CRANE ★ ILLUSTRATED BY CHRIS ELLISON

For all readers who believe in true hearts,
honor, and promises to keep.
—CAROL

❧

In memory of my grandparents:
Irma Mae Bueto Austin, Mary Virginia Ellison,
and Jewel Collins Ellison.
—CHRIS

Sleeping Bear Press™

315 East Eisenhower Parkway, Suite 200
Ann Arbor, MI 48108
www.sleepingbearpress.com

© 2011 Sleeping Bear Press, a part of Cengage Learning.

10 9 8 7 6 5 4 3 2 1

Library of Congress Cataloging-in-Publication Data
The Christmas tree ship / written by Carol Crane; illustrated by Chris Ellison.
p. cm.
ISBN 978-1-58536-285-1
1. Michigan, Lake, Region—History—Juvenile literature. 2. Christmas trees—Michigan,
Lake, Region—History—Juvenile literature. 3. Schuenemann, Herman, d. 1912—Juvenile
literature. 4. Rouse Simmons (Schooner)—Juvenile literature. I. Ellison, Chris, ill. II. Title.
F553.C73 2011
977.4—dc22

Printed by China Translation & Printing Services Limited,
Guangdong Province, China. 1st printing. 07/2011

When Tim and I were boys, we lived with Grandpa Axel and Grandma Hannah in a lighthouse on Lake Michigan. We both loved to help Grandpa Axel with his job as a lighthouse keeper. I would carry Grandpa's toolbox so he could check the light and test the foghorn. Many times a ship passing by would toot its horn and the crew would wave to us. I especially loved it when the sailors saluted us.

Grandpa taught us all about the water. He told us that Lake Michigan is like a child with many moods.

"Sometimes the mood is very, very good, and sometimes it's very, very bad." Grandpa could tell if a storm was brewing just by feeling the wind. "Wait long enough," he'd tell us, "and the weather will change with the wind."

One day, just before Christmas, I could tell a storm was on its way. The crisp air had turned damp. The water near shore had become a dark, greenish-colored froth. Black clouds quickly began to roll in. Tim and I figured that the lake sure was in a bad mood!

Grandpa hurried us inside the warm kitchen before we got soaked. Grandma Hannah was baking a batch of her sweet-smelling ginger cookies, and my cousins were setting out glasses for milk.

Grandpa Axel then sat down in his story rocker. It was a hand-carved chair, one he had brought with him from Sweden. My cousins, Tim, and I gathered close to the chair.

We each had our favorite story, but mine was the story of the Christmas Tree Ship. It must have been one of Grandpa's favorites, too, because he looked toward me, then smiled and winked as he picked up his carving and began speaking slowly, weaving again the tale I so loved.

"Every year Captain Santa would load up his little schooner *Rouse Simmons* with thousands of beautiful Christmas trees from our northern Michigan forests. Now, you children know the lake, and you know how stormy it is in November. But every year Captain Santa braved the weather to bring those trees to the children of Chicago.

This year he had told his wife Barbara that this was the final trip. He was growing old, and the *Rouse Simmons* was growing old, and as much as he loved selling, and sometimes giving away, those Christmas trees, this year was going to be his last.

He and his crew set off across the lake with five thousand trees, all bundled tightly in the hold and lashed to the deck. The captain had sailed the lake all his life, and he knew when a storm was coming. He felt the wind change, he felt the dampness in the air, and he had all the sails hoisted to race that storm across the lake. But the wind blew harder and harder, and the sleet, ice, and snow covered that little schooner and her trees and eventually pulled her under the water."

Then the schooner slowly slipped
beneath the churning lake.
Lost were the captain and his crew,
this Christmas Ship heartbreak.

Grandpa got up and walked over to the window.

"If you could see straight across the lake," he told us, "you'd see the shores of Wisconsin. A little to the south would be Two Rivers, Wisconsin, very near where the ship went down. After that storm, the winds from the southwest washed driftwood and treasures from the *Rouse Simmons* clear across the lake and onto our Michigan shores. I have something to show you," said Grandpa. "The waves buried it in the sand for quite a few years, but the wind uncovered it."

Grandpa pulled something out of his pocket. It was a corroded tag that said: Chicago Market, 1912.

"These copper straps were used to bundle Christmas trees together," he told us. Grandpa said that after the *Rouse Simmons* went down, some of the trees were found, still in their bundles. "We pulled the trees out of the lake. In honor of the captain, everyone helped put a tree up on the lighthouse for all to see."

"The next year the children of Chicago were sad. Captain Santa would not arrive at the pier. But then, something wonderful happened: there, in the same spot, was another schooner laden with beautiful Christmas trees."

Miraculously, the next year
an old schooner did appear.
Moored at the same spot with trees,
who had anchored it here?

The Captain's wife, Barbara,
and her daughters had decided,
the Christmas Tree Ship tradition would live on.
Somehow trees would be provided.

For the brave heart of her husband,
recalling his true dedication,
she brought trees from the north—
a deed of respect and admiration.

Grandpa had finished telling the old story. Every year, one of Grandpa's carvings was hung on our Christmas tree. Eagerly waiting, we wiggled in anticipation of who would be chosen to add the wooden carving. That year I got to hang the ornament—a replica of Captain Santa's schooner that once carried Christmas trees to Chicago.

AUTHOR'S NOTE

Local newspaper accounts and other sources tell us that the *Rouse Simmons*, a Great Lakes schooner, was built in 1868 in Milwaukee, Wisconsin. In late November of 1912 the ship was carrying more than 5,000 fresh-cut evergreen trees from Michigan's Upper Peninsula town of Thompson, near Manistique, to Chicago, Illinois. Captain Herman Schuenemann was known to have sold the Christmas trees for many years dockside at the Chicago River's Clark Street docks for fifty cents or one dollar each or to have given them away to poor families. Shortly before the ship set sail, Captain Schuenemann, who had been given the nickname Captain Santa, had promised his wife that this would be the last run on the aging schooner.

Sadly, the *Rouse Simmons* never completed the planned last voyage across the lake. A storm with gale force winds and snow moved across the water and is believed to have taken the ship down. Remains of the schooner were found in 1971 near Two Rivers, Wisconsin, in 172 feet of water. Christmas trees were still neatly stacked and strapped to the ship's deck. Items recovered from the *Rouse Simmons* wreckage are part of a shipwreck collection in the Rogers Street Fishing Village Museum in Two Rivers. In 2007 the shipwreck of the *Rouse Simmons* was listed on the National Register of Historic Places.

The events of this story are fiction, based on fact. My grandfather, Axel Anderson, loved to tell stories. I would sit with my cousins and listen to his many tales of Michigan. He had emigrated to the United States from Sweden with his new wife Hannah in 1882. The upper portion of lower Michigan must have reminded my grandfather of Sweden with its lakes, trees, and rolling hills. They settled in the

CAPTAIN
HERMAN SCHUENEMANN

Frankfort area, and Grandfather took on jobs such as log setter, fisherman, and lighthouse signal repairman. As he shared his stories with us, Grandfather Anderson sat in his rocking chair—the one he had brought from Sweden in a bag and put back together piece by piece. He fondly called it his "remembering rocker." It was the only possession he had brought with him to America.

I cherish my memories of Grandfather's stories, told with his Swedish accent, often around a campfire. I especially loved hearing his story of Captain Schuenemann bringing trees to waiting families in Chicago—and my grandfather did find trees scattered along the Michigan shoreline, bound with copper tags from the *Rouse Simmons*. My summers were spent on Lake Michigan, and looking out across this large expanse of sparkling water, I often wondered if at some time another girl on the Wisconsin shore could be waving at me standing on the Michigan shore.

—*Carol Crane*

CAROL CRANE

Carol Crane loves to write about her family. *The Christmas Tree Ship* is based on a story Carol's Swedish grandfather told of bravery and the dedication of a Lake Michigan ship's captain and his family. Carol and her cousins spent their summers on the shores of Lake Michigan swimming, boating, and fishing. She also picked cherries to earn money for school clothes in the fall.

She is often asked by children during school visits what inspired her to become a writer. Her answer is, "Reading other authors' words about their experiences. I have spent many hours at the library using books as a vehicle for traveling all over the world."

Carol's previous book, *The Handkerchief Quilt*, is about her mother, who was a reading teacher who brought the community together to sew a quilt made from handkerchiefs given to her by her students. Carol now resides in North Carolina with her two grandsons and their two cats, Dali and Skittles, who listen to her stories.

CHRIS ELLISON

Chris Ellison received his formal art training at the Harris School of Art in Franklin, Tennessee, and later at the Portfolio Center in Atlanta, Georgia. He has illustrated both children's picture books and adult historical fiction for more than 20 years. Chris has illustrated several books for Sleeping Bear Press including *Pappy's Handkerchief* and *Let Them Play*, both named Notable Social Studies Trade Books for Young People. Chris lives in Mississippi with his wife, Lesley, and two young sons.